Everything We Ever Saw

From the Beach to the Bush and MORE!

Roland Harvey

ALLEN&UNWIN
SYDNEY • MELBOURNE • AUCKLAND • LONDON

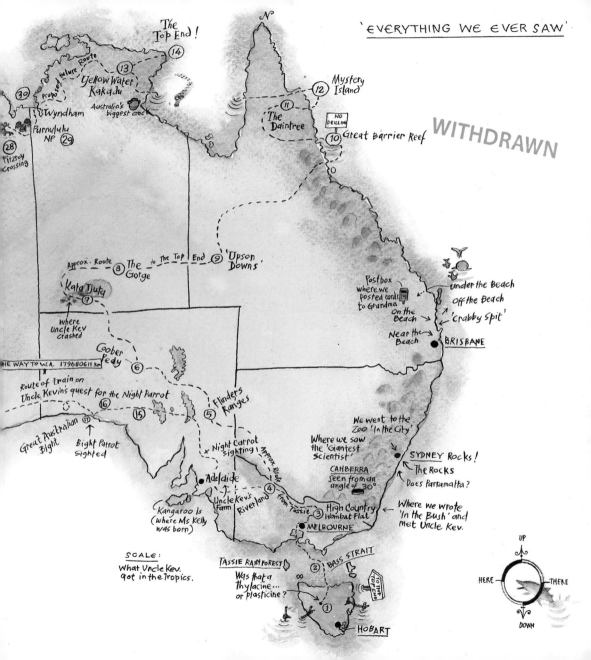

At the BEACH

Postcards from Crabby Spit

AT LAST I'M OFF to Crabby Spit!
Now... have I got everything?
I'm not going to LOSE anything this year...

easel

stool

brush

phone

sunnies

umbrella

hat

sandals

binoculars

camera

towel

paints

backpack

Ha!

secret tunnel to surf beach

farm house where we hired the horses

Footbridge

bike path

Secret graves

Haunted house

ghost tree

Canoe tree

bike path

Mr. Sing's cabbage farm

surf shop

Ice Cream Shop

surf cafe

Butcher

Pub

SPIT STREET

cafe

Dance Hall

Treasure Trove

Hundred Cabbage Road

Cinema

surfboard factory

surf shop

tool shed

Sand Pit

The big tree

school

vegie garden

Boat Hire

Boat Builders

Boat Builders

Hardware

Fish & Chips

Hot Bread

Grocers

ground

toilets

BBQ

route of the ice cream van

car park

Store

"Crabby's" Backpackers

Bus Station

Petrol

tennis wall

Deep End

Crabby Pool

Police

Fire stn

our camp

bike path

Sea Scouts

site of bonfire ✗

beach

Slipway

Yacht Club of Crabby Spit

Kiosk

Park

PARK

To the outside world

I saw the glow-in-the-dark crab!

Rotunda

cliff walk

Playground

BOWLS CLUB

Bowl →

Swimming Beach

channel

moorings

Ferry

MAP OF

CRABBY SPIT

FROM THE SURVEY BY

ROLAND B HARVEY ESQ. 1957

SCALE: SIMILAR TO JOCK ITCH. ONLY WORSE

Mussel farm

under water at high tide

heathland wildflower reserve

unstable cliffs

Bluff ave

Meteorite Crater

Lookout tower

For Frankie

Goodbye, my darlings!
Don't forget to write!

Rajah

Frankie

At the BEACH

Postcards from Crabby Spit

Roland Harvey

Goodbye Grandma! Goodbye!

Henry

Dad

Mum

Penny

Pierre

Welcome to
CRABBY SPIT

Dear Grandma

We are nearly at Crabby Spit! On the way we had to stop 3 times and Frankie was sick 4 times. We saw a policeman and he told dad to speed up because he was holding up traffic.

We saw a monster in a lake and I saw 12 baby ducks and 2 giant crabs.

Rajah found a towel beside the road! I can't wait to get to Crabby Spit. I drew us for you. Love from Henry

Dad

Rajah

Mum

Penny

Henry

Frankie

Dear Grandma, Crabby Spit is COOL! We have the best camping spot right near the toilets and the beach and the river. Mum has agreed to stop embarrassing us and only wear her new hat in the tent if we do ALL the cooking for the whole holiday. One family has brought their mower and we are getting fish and chips for tea and then going looking for crabs. There is a bike track and a river and horse riding and mosquitoes.

Love from Henry

Dear Grandma ... WOW!! It's all happening at Crabby. Dad says the lifesavers are wanting him to join the club and Mr. MacIntosh was chased by a shark. It must have been scared off by the taste of his shorts. And I saw a bird drop a poo on a kid's hand. I'm going to join the lifesavers and row the surfboat and drive the rubber duckies. I tell you what, Grandma, surfing is ace. I am going to get really good and be world champ. There was a hang-glider and I want to be world champ of that too. That's after I get to be world champion at Frisbee. I drew this picture of a hang-glider for you!

♡ love ♡ Penny

Dear Grandma, We are having a good time here at Crabby Spit. At the Sand Sculpture Competition today Mrs. Thomas made Mr. Thomas into a mermaid and won! The kids helped dad build a sandcastle and Uncle Kevin is going to have another go at the surfboard. One kid thinks he is a seagull and a little dog did a wee on a lady's foot. Some people have been catching fish and they showed us how to clean them.

I have become a vegetarian. I don't know how the seagull kid does it. He only stays up for about 20 seconds so I think he's cheating.

♡ Penny

Hey Grandma! I couldn't find a pen so I had to use a stick dipped in paint. It is really pouring today so we went to Treasure Trove and bought some cool stuff. I wanted some 20m White Pointer jaws but got a snake instead. Mum bought dad an ironing board because he thinks he's Iron Man.

See ya, Henry

ALL WORK BY LOCAL ARTISTS

CRABBY OLD CLOTHES

Dear Grandma, I bet you would love Crabby Spit. It is so windy today that I saw some underpants fly across the camping ground. The last I saw they were on the back of a lady's head.

We played Scrabble in the annexe and had hot chocolate and marshmallow floaters. Afterwards we helped clean up the beach. Mr Thomas' stuff floated away yesterday and today the wind is blowing it all back again! Dad is going to buy a heap of fish and chips and invite everyone to a party!

I hope Frankie's mice and my axolotl are OK and not too much trouble.

♡ from Penny

DEAR GRANDMA

Mum is helping me write this postcard because she is very sunburnt and has to stay in the shade.
Uncle Pete and Auntie Sam came to visit and we beat them at beach cricket. Penny bowled Uncle Pete for a duck and I saw a snake. And I missed a catch because I was busy surfing.
Mum is teaching me to swim and I can put my face in the water right up to my chin.
Dad is cooking his big fish tonight!
bye FRANKIE

Dear Grandma

We have been floating down the river and doing bombs off Sentinel Rock in the estuary. When we were snorkelling in the rockpool we saw seven starfish and a leafy seadragon and I drew you one. You almost can't tell they're not seaweed. I think dad has sunstroke because he dressed in seaweed and danced in front of everyone. It was _so_ embarrassing.

A kid called James had sore feet and our friend made him sandals out of kelp!   bye for now,   Penny

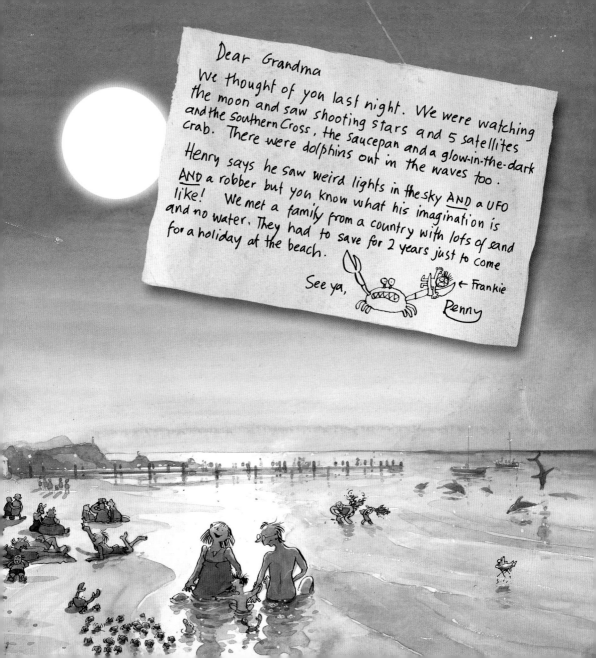

Dear Grandma, Today was the <u>BEST</u> day, we went diving again in the DEEP water and found SUNKEN TREASURE and SHIPWRECKS and a STINGRAY and an OCTOPUS and a GIANT CLAM!

I drew you a map so you can find the treasure if you come down to Crabby Spit. You will have to <u>be careful</u> because I think there will be things guarding it. And traps.

Good Luck. Love,

Henry

Cliffs

shallow

→ To Crabby spit

Deep Water

sand

rock

X

Dear Grandma
How are your holidays going? Today mum took us
sailing and dad was worried so Frankie and I
worked the sails. We went out to an island and
saw a really dark cave which I think would have
been used by pirates!
Yee hee hee and a nice cup of tea!
we picked up a whole lot of rubbish in the water and
we also found out seagulls like eating sick. It probably
has more flavour than plastic or chips. We saw 4 dolphins
and one looked right at me.
One looked a bit like
Auntie Joy.
love from Henry

Dear Grandma, We had a _real_ adventure today!
We hired bikes and rode all around Crabby Spit.
Frankie said he saw a crocodile and I saw pelicans
and swamphens and Hannah Colman. They were
catching fish and eating them whole. YUCK!!!

And after lunch we went HORSERIDING
and now dad won't sit down. He
said his horse needed new springs.
He was being the man from Snowy
River and nearly fell into the water.

This is my invention. Do you
think I'll get rich? xxxx Penny

I can't draw

spring seat

shocks!

roll-up ladder

Hey Grandma! We have been on a ferry today to Skull Island. It is huge when you get close and smells like Henry's room because of all the bird poo. I don't think humans have ever been onto it! The sides are SO steep and there's just a little jetty.

On the pier we saw a man catch a squid. He was teasing it and it suddenly squirted a whole lot of black ink in his face! Serves him right. The man gave the squid to dad and I have a weird feeling dad thinks we're going to eat it. I'm having calamari from the shop, instead. I think I saw a giant octopus under the pier camouflaged as seaweed.
Hope you're having fun too! My hair looks like this →

love, Penny

Dear Grandma, It is so NOT good it's our last Crabby Spit night!! We had a humungous bonfire on the beach and people got dressed up and sang and drummed and danced. we were HOT! ♡ Penny

Dear Grandma I have never seen such a big fire and we toasted marshmallows. I think even some of the grownups had a good time. It was so cool with the sea slooshing and the music jumping. I made up a dance and my head stayed still and my body danced around. My dad was being funny and he's done his back.
Love from Henry

DEAR GRANDMA I stayed up late and there was a very big fire. I found a crab. And there were dolphins swimming in the sea. LOVE. FRANKIE

In the
BUSH

Henry

Penny

Mum

Dad

Frankie

Walking track to Equator and Northern Hemisphere

Mt. Misery 1999 m

Mt. No-name (submerged) 1821

The Jigsaw

where we skied

Where the Yeti was

Gully of Quiet Whispers

The High Plateau

Mt. Great Concern

1821 Max Flood Level

The Bluff

Hut where we slept when the snow came

x First snowball

where Uncle Kevin skied the cliff!

UP DOWN

Roaring Meg

Hidden Valley

cliffs

Hidden Valley sign

N (N=Nowhere)

World's second-tallest tree

old track to Hidden Valley

Gate

Sunset

Sunrise

Bagpipe Man

Where Rose Red saved the little rooster from the wicked Yeti

clearing

S (S=somewhere)

Black Gorge

Camp II x

Our campfire

Walking track

To the sea →

Hut

rapids

River Crossing

Flying Fox

Professor's secret hideout

Where we saw the trout jump

old jail

Police Paddock

old Cemetery

old sports oval

FEATHERTAIL FLATS

Site of the old Town

of old painter the faraway hills

MAP   OF

WOMBAT FLAT

and the very

HIGH PLAINS

FROM THE ORIGINAL SURVEY BY ROLAND
1066 – 7

→ 1 litre

0   1 CUP   2 CUPS   3 CUPS   4 CUPS   5 CUPS   6 CUPS   7 CUPS

NOTES: MAGNETIC NORTH CAN ATTRACT IRON FILINGS AND OFTEN INCREASES IN DEPTH PARTICULARLY DURING HEAVY SNOW. TRAVELLERS SHOULD CONSULT CURRENT DOCUMENTS AND OBTAIN LOCAL INFORMATION AT ALL TIMES, ESPECIALLY DURING FOG.

For Herbie

In the
BUSH

Our Holiday at Wombat Flat

Roland Harvey

7.03 AM

Hi, I'm Henry and I can't wait to get to Wombat Flat!

Hi, I'm Penny and I can't wait to go horseriding!

Hi, I'm Mum and I can't wait to get out of this car!

Hi, I'm Dad and I can't wait to see Uncle Kev's new canoe!

Hi, I'm Frankie

and I can't wait to go to the toilet...

Penny saw a Wedge-tailed Eagle's nest.

Mum said Wombats have four-wheel drive

but only one speed.

Dad wanted a campsite with...

No branches (over)
roots (under)
hoons (near)
ants (in)
smells (around)
puddles (about)

Penny

We arrived at Wombat Flat in time for breakfast...

...behind some people collecting firewood.

The first people we saw were the Smiths from school.

Smith!

Mr Smith showed us a rare kangaroo orchid.

Mum reckons some people don't know how to pack a trailer.

the road to Snowy Bluff → Horse yard

Toilets   old graves

the road to Snakey Flat →   Eagle's nest

From the City →

River

where we saw the Smiths ×

log Crossing   The Pool   The Falls   Hut

The Map of Wombat Flat

Uncle Kevin tested his new canoe.

Flat hair

Henry
the Titanic
I can't wait to enter the Great Boat Race!

Uncle Kev struck GOLD...

and I went panning for gold.

A mob of kangaroos came down to the river for a drink.

And a swarm of hoons set up camp next to us.

Dad said we should move camp to a quieter spot.

Frankie found a frog under the tent.

Start of The Great Boat Race

x ← Where Uncle Kev found gold

Where we panned for gold

our camp

The cascades

x Camp of Svlad the tiger doctor

the hoons camp

The Red Bluff

The Black Hole

Map of our First camp

N

Some walkers have found a bushrangers' hideout near Moonlight's Gap!

THE HIP REPLACEMENTS

Frankie

Today we are going Caving at Bushrangers' Hideout!

To Wombat Flat ←

Byrne's Lookout

7.5 km

Kelly's Bridge

Cliffs

Secret Cave

321 m

River

Mt Tenir 2136 m.

We saw stalactites

and stalagmites

and a stalagmightn't

I hid from Dad behind a rock and could hear laughing under the ground!

We found some old drawings...

Uncle Kev thinks there's a secret entrance to a hidden cavern...

Secret Entrance

but we couldn't find one.

The most exciting thing in the cave was a tiny frog with a smiley face.

Henry

We cooked
potatoes in
the hot coals
of the fire.

Mum told us to
look out for
wombats in the
evening.

Frankie met
Reggie Cray.

Ahh...
Dinner!

Uncle Kev and Dad told stories around the fire.

Dad said there were Feathertailed Gliders about but we didn't see any.

Uncle Kev is taking us white water rafting.

Penny

I jumped off the big rock five times and still didn't touch the bottom.

Good bomb

Bad bomb

Very Bad bomb

Uncle Kev
borrowed a canoe
and ...

... went over
Dead Man's Falls...

Dad thought
he saw a platypus.

Dead Man's
Falls

Uncle
Kev

Rapids

Cliff

Falls

Tunnel Bend

The
Tunnel

The
Pool

To Wombat
Flat

and possible
Monster

Penny

It was still dark when we
got up to saddle the horses...

We set off through
the morning mist...

... past the last
campers...

the horses had
a spell at Moonlight
Pass.

The sun was setting
as we neared the hut.

Henry's horse
was called
squid.

...up the long ridge
towards the bluff.

Dad

We made it
to the hut
just on
dark...

The sky was clear
and
it was really COLD.

We saw Orion's Belt
and the Dog Star!

We could see the lights of
Wombat Flat down in the valley.

Rigel
(Ry-jel)

☆ Sirius
(The dog star)

the Saucepan
(part of Orion)

the Milky
Way

Orion's
Belt

☆
Aldebaran

☆ Betelgeuse

Map of the Stars

scale: 1 cm = 1 billion billion miles

Frankie counted
three shooting stars
and seven satellites.

Mum

We were all a bit stiff and sore in the morning...

but still we were up to see the sunrise on the mountain.

We had tea and chops and pancakes for breakfast.

The boys from the Termite Hills Uphill and Downhill Club set off on the last leg of their expedition to Mt Misery.

...and the North Eastern Harmonica Society celebrated the discovery of the rare Mountain Pygmy Orchid!

Map

Falls

The Razorback

Mt Misery

The West Face

x where Dad saw the Yeti (HA HA HA!)

Us

Hut

UP

The Route to Mt Misery

Hidden Valley →

Base Camp

From Black Jack's

N

Henry

Cool!
It started
SNOWING!
We stayed in
the hut two
more nights.

Frankie
called his snowman
JOCK.

Dad said Uncle Kev's
Commando training made
him a born leader!

Uncle Kev said
the High Country was
no place for wimps or
the incompetent...

Penny made
a new friend...

Mum has found
a bunch of old
Wombu ski Club
gear in the hut.
Tomorrow... up the
hill we go!

Mum

We all found
something to
fit, and hit
the slopes!

The Wombat Flat
Ski team arrived
for pre-season
training.

WEAR SUNNIES
WHEN VIEWING
THIS PAGE

We did
downhill...

8

the most
difficult slope...
the DOUBLE
DOUGHNUT.

Too bad... that last big jump...

...bindings couldn't handle it.

ON THE SKI SLOPES: GREEN GIVES WAY TO RED

DON'T EAT YELLOW SNOW

Lesson 1
Standing

Lesson 2
Stopping techniques.

Lesson 3
The slalom.

Frankie

Frankie ↓ Horse ↓

We made new friends riding!

I saw 2 koalas and a cocky's nest.

We had to cross the river on the horses!

We rode
high above
the river...

and as we
came down
into the valley
it got hotter...

...and hotter...

...and I couldn't wait
to hit the pool!

Mum got run over
by a canoe.

New boots

Henry

...and boys.

At the bush dance there were nice girls to dance with.

Uncle Kev did a groin doing hip hop.

Dad impressed the locals by dancing on the table

and a pavlova.

Some people were doing the Windmill.

Mr Coombes gave a demonstration with his stockwhip.

Frankie ate 2 pavlovas and 16 party pies and was sick in a lady's shoe.

Frankie

Our last night was SCARY! People dressed up and told spooky stories around the fire.

 Dad's was the best...

It was about how Rose Red saved the little rooster and his family from The Wicked Yeti!

 I was a chicken.

 Uncle Kev was the little rooster.

Book Book Book

BUCK
BOOK

We called out to the
little rooster ...

BEHIND YOU
BEHIND YOU

And we all lived happily ever after !

We've had the greatest adventures of all time.

These were our favourites.
What did you like best?

Dad:
Getting to know
the locals.

Frankie:
Learning to fly.

Henry:
Leaping the Gap at
Mt Great Concern.

Penny:
The last
jump on the
Double Doughnut.

Mum:
The dance of the
Passionfruit Pavlova.

In the
CITY

5.15 a.m.

6 a.m.

To my mum,
who's ninety-seven
and was my
inspiration to draw

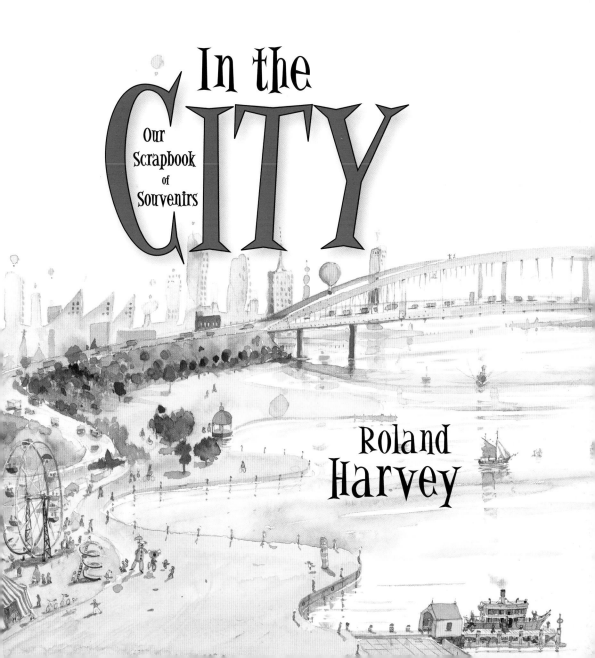

In the

Our Scrapbook of Souvenirs

CITY

Roland Harvey

Frankie

As we came over the bridge in the shuttle bus, we saw the top of the world's tallest building disappearing into the clouds...and the beach and a Peregrine Falcon and people playing tennis and Luna Park and the zoo and the aquarium.

I saw people going to work

and people going home...

And people parking their cars in the middle of the road.

Dad says there are 3,425,763 people in the city...and us!

The shuttle bus took us to the world's best hotel: the Grand Palace!

I can't wait to go to the aquarium.

Henry

Uncle Kev says the best way to get the feel of a city is to do a sewer tour... especially when it's raining.

There are hundreds of kilometres of tunnels under the city...

People even live there!

There are tunnels to take cars and trains and gas pipes and power lines and phone lines and water pipes and for people, animals, exhaust fumes, storm water and fresh air.

Sewage goes in as poo and comes out as water for factories and wildlife ponds.

Frankie was scared that all the storm water would wash the fish out of the aquarium before we got there.

At an 'historic dig' site I bought a dinosaur tooth necklace made from very early plastic.

Penny

The city square was weird at first, but we soon got the hang of it...Uncle Kev said we can go everywhere we want by bus, train, tram and bike, except the toilet.

12.17p.m. We have seen 3,425,740 people already and a dragon.

We saw university students having coffee and sharing a bowl of pasta.

We bought a T-shirt each and some tricks from a magic shop, but mine disappeared.

It was SO hot today and we went to the COOLEST play at the kids' theatre and then had fish and chips for dinner. Frankie played, 'I want to be a big bad shark,' on the pool-o-phone.

I kept a bottle of shampoo and some shower caps as souvenirs. And a piece of special Grand Palace toilet paper.

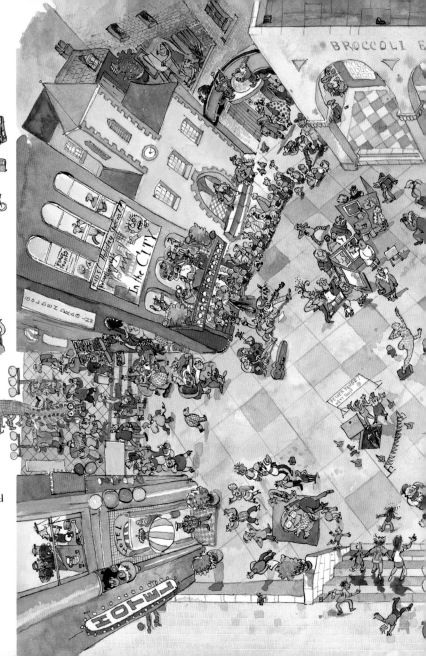

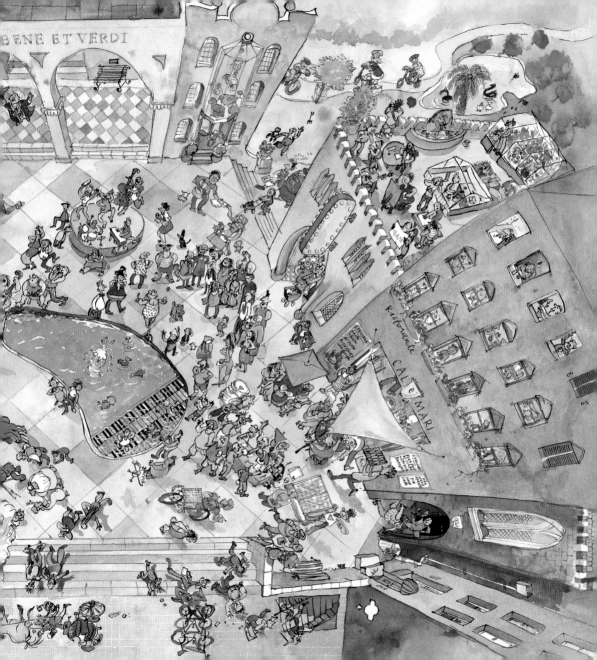

Henry

Our excursion today was to the biggest store in town. I saw some mannequins without any clothes on.

SCRAPBOOK NEWS FLASH

SHOPPERS IN THE CITY WERE SHOCKED TODAY WHEN A TERRIBLE TWO-HEADED BEAST ESCAPED FROM CHANGING ROOMS AND TERRORISED SHOPPERS BEFORE BEING TOLD TO LEAVE THE SHOP.

SIZE 61

Frankie and I got squashed in the lift and Penny nearly got crushed in the rush at a book launch.

Frankie said he could see the aquarium from Uncle Kev's office.

Dad and Mum took us for lunch on the roof at Raf's Caf and then picked up a crazy Kombi-board in the Bargain Basement.

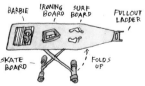

BARBIE   IRONING BOARD   SURF BOARD   PULLOUT LADDER

SKATE BOARD   FOLDS UP

Penny

Zoo checklist:

CATS
- [ ] Tigers
- [ ] Lions
- [ ] Ocelots
- [ ] Leopards
- [ ] Pumas
- [ ] Corgis

NOCTURNAL ANIMALS

MARSUPIALS

PRIMATES
- [ ] Gorillas
- [ ] Orang-utans
- [ ] Oranges
- [ ] Chimpanzees
- [ ] Uncle Kev

ENDANGERED ANIMALS
- [ ] Polar Bears
- [ ] Pandas
- [ ] Animals starting with 'x'

MONOTREMES

BEARS

SEALISH ANIMALS

LONG ANIMALS
- [ ] Giraffes
- [ ] Pythons
- [ ] Goannas
- [ ] Dachshunds

Frankie was disappointed there weren't any sharks.

My souvenir was a really cute little baby Taipan* I found in the toilets.

*Mum said I had to hand it in at the gate.

Henry

The market is the smelliest place in the world.

It has fishy smells, and **MARKET** mango and banana and old cabbage and herbs and coffee.

We saw a huge crab and tiny silver fish and squid with long tentacles and different coloured prawns and people.

Penny didn't like the meat section because she suffers from Vegetaria. I liked the way the butchers shouted at Mum and Dad. There was stuff even I was allergic to, like gizzards.

I snuck anchovies into Uncle Kev's back pocket.

We bought bread, prawns, nuts, coriander dip, and cow's cheese, goat's cheese, sheep's cheese, lychees and stinky cheese.

Frankie got lost and we found him at the big fish stall.

I got an excellent cheesy souvenir.

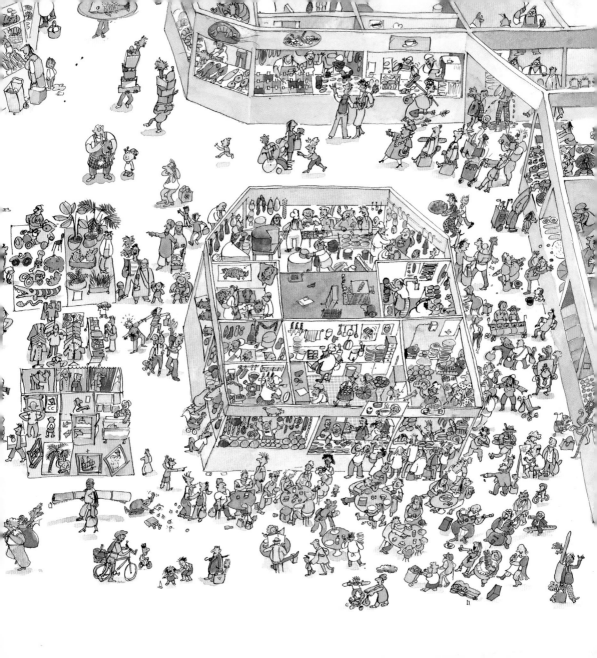

Penny

The Esplanade is where cool people go so you can see them, but Uncle Kev took us anyway as a special treat.

PEOPLE WERE:
Surfing
Cycling
Blading
Watching
Para-surfing   Sailboarding
Kite flying   Jogging
Sleeping
Frisbeeing
Walking
Lying Down

Uncle Kev had a sailboarding lesson and we got to ride in the Rescue Boat.

Mum had raspberry and mango ice-cream. I had beetroot and licorice. Dad had chicken ripple and baci. Frankie had mudcake and Henry had prawn and banana.

Frankie found a crab, but it didn't swim away when he put it in the water, so he kept it as a souvenir.

Henry

Carlington is old and cool. There are bookshops, bike shops, bakeshops, back shops, galleries, cafes, second-hand bookshops, restaurants, gourmet food shops, cookbook shops, arty bookshops and outside toilets.

Uncle Kev's breakdown van broke down.

Penny bought an op-shop wig that makes her look like the Queen.

We walked down the cobbled lanes where they used to take the little cart and empty all the toilets.

Frankie found an antiquarium bookshop.

I found my souvenir at a second-hand bookshop: The Boys' Own Annual from 1946.

Frankie

6.15a.m. We went up in a

HOT AIR BALLOON

people · basket · burner · fan · man · envelope

up ↑ · down ↓ · wind → · direction of travel → · FINISH ✗

Uncle Kev explained how it worked.

When the balloon was going up it roared like a dragon and when it was floating down it was SILENT!

Penny saw a frightened swan.

Henry saw a skate park.

I saw a fox and undies on a washing line and a big fish out of water and a submarine.

We each got a certificate.

BALLOON ADVENTURER

This is to certify that Frankie has successfully completed a hot air balloon flight from

Henry

We went to the toilet at the top of the highest building in the city. It has a glass wall and we could see very strange things...

...like a cinema on the roof!

...and a Peregrine falcon

...and a Peregrine falcon's eggs!

...and a Peregrine shorts

...and window-cleaners!

...and an artist's studio

...and vegie gardens

...and tennis courts

...and Frankie said he could see the aquarium.

We went up and down in the lift eleven times. The tenth time, Dad pushed the buttons for all the floors and a lady got cross.

I found a feather and made a souvenir pen and wrote a letter.

Penny

5 a.m.
I heard sirens and woke up really early.

Henry and I snuck up to the tower at the top of the hotel. We could see flashing lights and smoke and a baker's truck delivering bread, and milk trucks delivering milk,

rubbish trucks delivering rubbish,

water trucks delivering water and burglar trucks collecting burglars

and joggers collecting blisters and a powerful owl.

Frankie slept through the whole thing.

I kept the front page of the newspaper showing the fire.

THE
NEWS
HUGE FIRE
DAMAGES HISTORIC
SHED

Henry

The most amazing exhibit at the museum was the giant scientist. We went into his mouth, down his oesophagus...and watched his heart beating 1,2,3 – 1,2,3 – his lungs wheezing and his bowels squeezing.

We even got samples.

I didn't know Indigenous people lived without shops and mobile phones for 50,000 years and they invented barbecues and boats and made mummies before the Egyptians.

Dad said there was a live 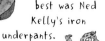 chameleon in the museum but they can't find it!

The bit I liked best was Ned Kelly's iron underpants.

I bought a 3-D pop-up model of the city.

Penny

We went to the oldest part of town which was built before man was invented or cars or electricity or pyjamas.

We saw old stuff like pots and pipes and china and bones and shoes and pistols and dead rats and mugs and T-shirts with pictures of an opera house.

 This postcard was from when everything was black and white.

There is a kids' gallery with dress-ups and DVDs of the olden days and you can be an orphan and I saw a chimney-sweep and convicts!

It felt like we had gone back in time, so we had lunch. Frankie was quiet all day – he was saving his energy for tomorrow.

I got a souvenir koala and a photo of some people we don't know.

Frankie

The aquarium! HOORAY!

I saw lots of fish
starting with 's':
sharks, stingrays,
salmon, scallops,
salamanders, sashimi, sea-
snakes, sea slugs, sandwiches
of tuna, sardines,
shrimps, sperm whales,
socktopus, and
a big barracuda.

The divers swam
with the huge sharks
and FED them.

We put our heads in the
bubble and it felt like we
were fish too.

The best animals in
the world are the
leafy sea dragons.

I found out that
barracuda eat anchovies.

Anchovies eat plankton.

Whales and shrimp eat
plankton, too.

Leafy sea dragons eat shrimp and
plankton. They don't eat whales.

I hope nothing eats
leafy sea dragons.

Sharks eat
whatever
they like.

NIGHT, OWEN.
SEE YOU AT
THE PUB LATER

NUH...
I'VE GOT
HOCKEY
PRACTICE.
NITE
PHIL

STAGE
DOOR

STAFF
EXIT
PLEASE USE
MAIN ENTRANCE

We had fun in the city...

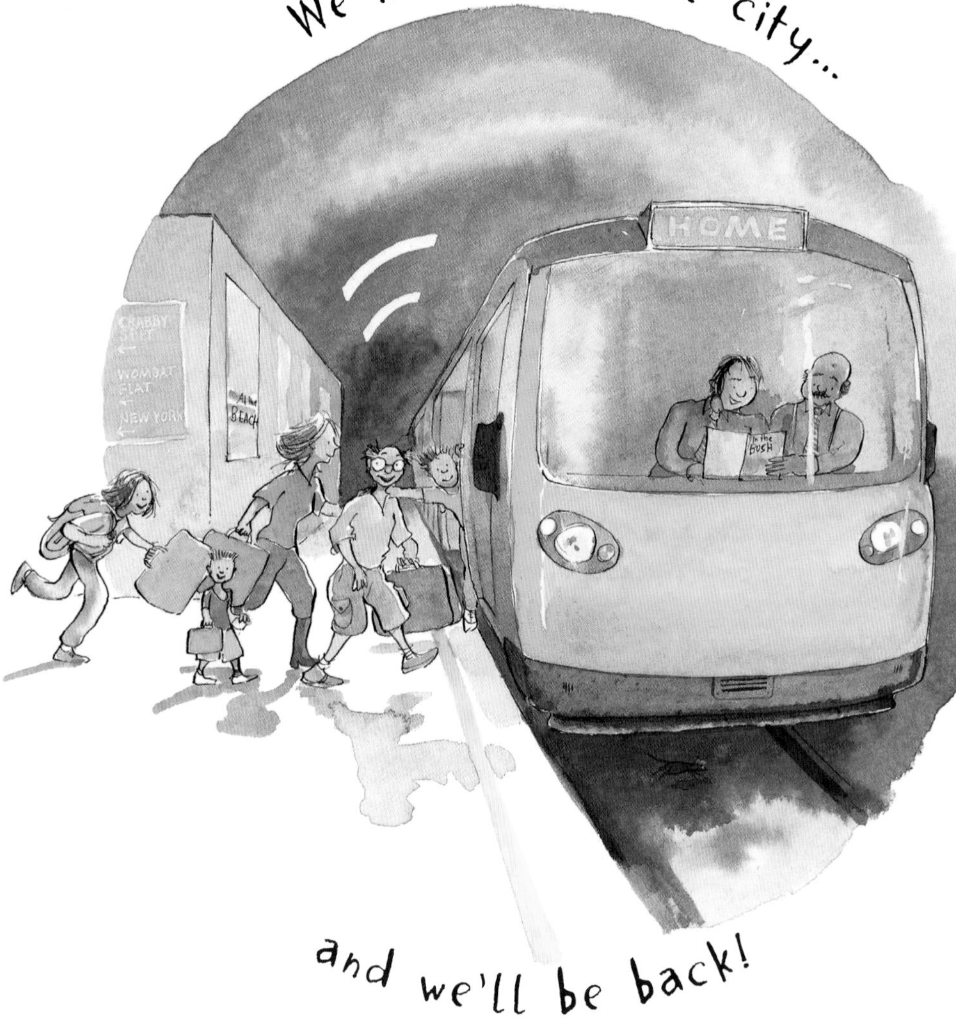

and we'll be back!

To the
TOP END

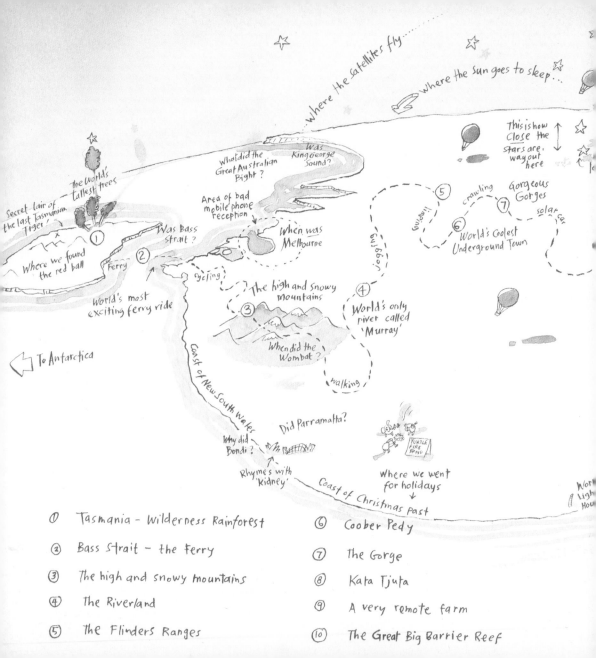

Where the satellites fly.....

Where the sun goes to sleep...

This is how Close the stars are way out here

the World's tallest trees

Secret lair of the last Tasmanian Tiger?

Where we found the red ball

What did the Great Australian Bight?

Was King George Sound?

Area of bad mobile phone reception

When was Melbourne

crawling

Gorgeous Gorges

⑦

solar car

⑤

⑥

World's Coolest Underground Town

Was Bass Strait?

Ferry

②

①

cycling

The high and snowy mountains

③

④

World's only river called 'Murray'

jogging

World's most exciting ferry ride

When did the Wombat?

walking

To Antarctica

Coast of New South Wales

Did Parramatta?

Why did Bondi?

Rhymes with 'Kidney'

TURTLE FIRE POND

Where we went for holidays

Coast of Christmas past

Worl Ligh Hou

① Tasmania - Wilderness Rainforest

② Bass Strait - the Ferry

③ The high and snowy mountains

④ The Riverland

⑤ The Flinders Ranges

⑥ Coober Pedy

⑦ The Gorge

⑧ Kata Tjuta

⑨ A very remote farm

⑩ The Great Big Barrier Reef

Edge of the World as we know it...

Here is Proof that the earth is flat
x

ar

flying doctor

Last petrol for 10 000 km.

e Kev
s his ultralight's steering....

What did Darwin?

Where we saw crocs and met Owen Peli...

What did Kakadu?

⑬ Where did Arnhem Land?

horses

Where we met the Chooky Dancers and mum ate a raw oyster, really + truly.

⑨ World's most remote farm

World's most interesting wall

camel

balloon

World's largest Crocodile!

⑭ The Top

BIRD INFORMATION:
• Can a Magpie Lark?
• Can a Barnswallow?
• Can a Caspian Tern?
• No, But a Pelican.

Why should a Cassowary?

Where Uncle Kev ate greenants!

Did the Pacific Black Duck?

Why did the butterfly?

⑪ walked

the Tip
⇨ to P.N.G

swam

⑫ We saw a dugong and some ladies kayaking...

Home of the 'White Pointer' sandfly

⑩ Where we went diving

Where the moon comes from

⑪ Daintree Rainforest Wilderness

⑫ Mystery Island

⑬ Kakadu

⑭ The Tip top!

South   North → Far North

SCALE: Doh Ray Me Fah So La Tee Doh

To the TOP END

Our trip across Australia

Roland Harvey

In the Wilderness, Uncle Kevin used his Commando training to take some people white-water rafting...

He said that here in the rainforest there are wombats...

Dad showed us the safe way to cross a log bridge...

Some trees are so tall they could touch the clouds...

...rosellas

...Tassie Devils...

...but...

and no Thylacines...

... and Frankie spotted fish.

In Bass Strait it was very rough and very windy... and Penny spent a lot of time feeding the

We saw dolphins and boats

we saw socks and undies

and we saw seals

and diving birds

and giant squid

and we would have seen sharks except they're scared of Uncle Kev...

fish and a dolphin stole our red ball and

Uncle Kev told us about giant sea creatures and it was SCARY.

But we don't believe him...

do we...

Dolphins swam around

our boat...

We saw a blue whale called 'Humpty' who had a calf

which we haven't named yet...

Uncle Kev told stories of giant creatures living in the depths, but they're not true

Bogong Jack's Hut is the noisiest place on the High Plains.

whisper
whisper

creak...
creak...

skreeearchhh...

aaarr...

rustle
rustle

In a deep dark damp gully a lyrebird sang a hundred songs of different birds

sigh

roarrr...

whinny

oooof

thwack
thwack

troarrr

neigh

oooh!

Croak
Croak

sploosh

plop

ssssshhh

swoosh

scrape

screech

Kaaaarrr..
aaaaarrr..r

thump

zzzzzzz..

rusty hinge
rusty hinge...

chirp
chirp

warble
warble

and on a distant mountainside, another answered...

..r whit

gurgle

mmmphh

bok bok bok
bok

Peeee...

ts..ts.ts..

In the Riverland...

I learned that in birdwatching...

....it pays to look where you are going

It was really hot paddling... so we visited a farm and bought oranges and peaches to eat on the riverbank.

On a jetty we met a dog who has his own scarf and goggles.

We saw emus but they're not really this big!

While we paddled Uncle Kev told us about the local bunyips. But we know Uncle Kev, he's only joking!

We had fish and chips on the old wharf.

Dad and I saw... ten swamphens nesting...

six pelicans...

three coots a-laying...

nine brolgas dancing...

two black swans...

30 different ducks...

and a yabbie in a dead tree!

BIG YABBIE

In the Flinders Ranges...

We saw sulphur-crested cockies

...and Red-tailed Black cockies

...it was hot and dry...

...except in the creek.

We hired bikes

to ride

the

very bumpy roa

.. and yellow-tailed

Black cockies, who fly funny...

... and some German people from Carlton.

... and some American people from Canada...!

and some American

We met some Japanese people from Japan...

Uncle Kev is a really clever rider!

Dad said to ride carefully or we'd get flat tyres...

up the gorge...

At Kata Tjuta, Uncle Kev went for

We played

Henry has such an imagination! He thinks one rock looks

hide

and

seek

like Uncle Kev, only smaller.

a test flight in his ultralight by doing a lap of the rocks.

Unfortunately, he started showing off...

Henry saw a mob of big red roos.

...and a pack of dingoes

...a gigabyte of budgies

...and a slither of lizards

...a circus of emus

...got lost...

and one lone eagle.

and around the rocks

A soaring wedgetail watched us all   from high above the cliffs

... I think...

I didn't want to dance in front
of my family. I went off to look for
water monsters, but they're just a myth...

On the road to
'Upson Downs'
Station ...

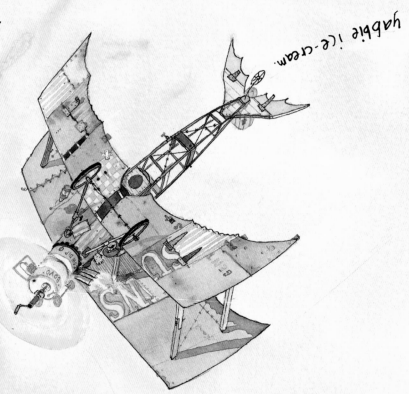

yabbie ice-cream.

Mr Murphy rolled the ute again on Saturday night...

on a very

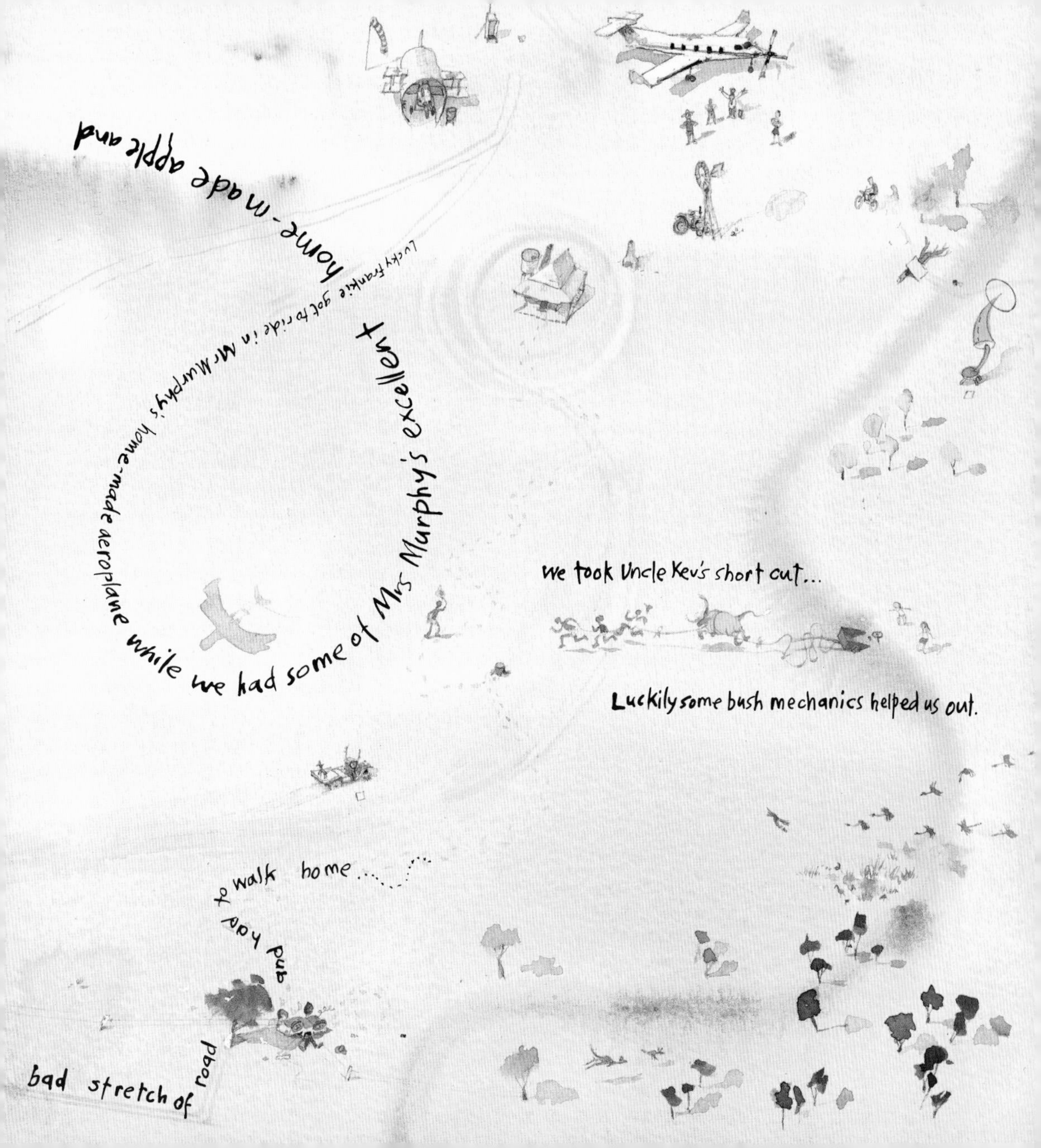

home-made apple and home-made aeroplane while we had some of Mrs Murphy's excellent

Lucky Frankie got to ride in Mr Murphy's home

we took Uncle Kev's short cut...

Luckily some bush mechanics helped us out.

& walk home....

bad pub

bad stretch of road

Uncle Kev guided the tour boat using his new GPS.

Some fish feed on the surface...

...dugong

...and shark.

...and some on the bottom.

Deep in the Daintree Rainforest Wilderness...

Turquoise

Swallowtailed

butterflies

A dragon scurried up a tree...

...and a butterfly

alighted on a vine.

Uncle Kev ate Green Ants!

flickered

about...

A brilliant Azure Kingfisher swooped low over the water...

At Mystery Island...

Uncle Kev showed us how to handle a racing cat.

We met some ladies who had paddled all the way from the mainland

A pod of dolphins played around the ferry.

People came from town to enjoy the solitude.

We fed fish

...and snorkelled around the reef...

and sat on the pure white sand.

to stay on the island.

Visiting boats anchor in the deeper water...

5:30 AM at Yellow Water and it is already hot.
We had a bird-spotting competition.
I saw 5 million birds, but
Frankie won with 32 billion.

We saw ducks fishing

and fish ducking

and waterlilies

and an eagle.

We saw turtles and salties and magpie geese and spoonbills...
...and a jabiru and brolgas and egrets and some Americans.

YAY! We made it from Tassie to the very tip of the TOP End...

and
it
floated
back
to
me
!

I kicked the ball to a brolga and she headed it to an emu but a kangaroo

... right out of Australia ...

and he kicked it

and he gave it to some dolphins and they

an uncle & passed it

and he gave it to some dolphins and they

she swam it out to a shark

hit it to a turtle and

Then we all sat down and had a campfire feast.

WISH YOU WERE HERE!

The Wilds of Tasmania

Sailing the high seas of lower Bass Strait

The High Country

The Murray River

Wallaby-spotting in the Flinders Ranges

Down-Under Coober Pedy

Picnic at Kata Tjuta

The Gorge

The Great Thirsty Desert

The Great Big Barrier Reef

Deep in the Daintree

Mystery Island

Crocs of Kakadu

Near the Tip of the Top End

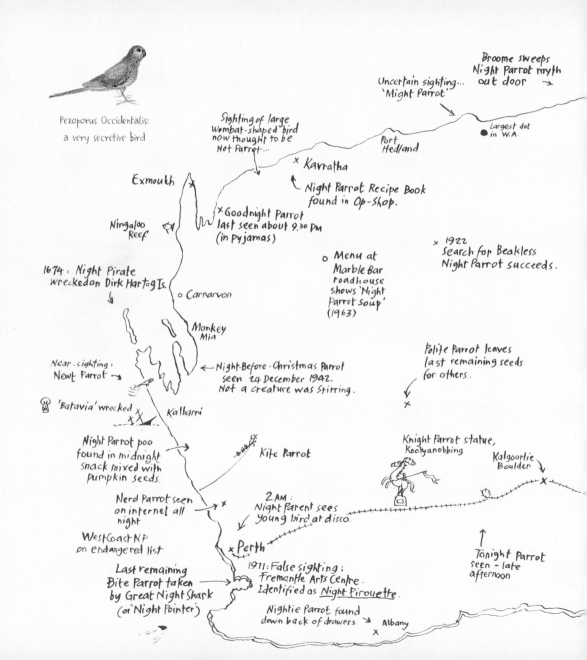

Pezoporus Occidentalis:
a very secretive bird

Broome sweeps
Night Parrot myth
out door →

Uncertain sighting...
'Might Parrot'

Largest dot
● in W.A.

Port
Hedland

Sighting of large
Wombat-shaped bird
now thought to be
Not Parrot...

x Karratha

↰ Night Parrot Recipe Book
found in Op-Shop.

Exmouth

Ningaloo
Reef

x Goodnight Parrot
last seen about 9.30 PM
(in pyjamas)

o Menu at
Marble Bar
roadhouse
shows 'Night
Parrot Soup'
(1963)

x 1922
Search for Beakless
Night Parrot succeeds.

1674: Night Pirate
wrecked on Dirk Hartog Is.
↓

o Carnarvon

Monkey
Mia

Polite Parrot leaves
last remaining seeds
for others.
↓
x

Near-sighting:
Newt Parrot →

← Night-Before-Christmas Parrot
seen 24 December 1942.
Not a creature was Stirring.

'Batavia' wrecked x
x x   Kalbarri

Night Parrot poo
found in midnight
snack mixed with
pumpkin seeds.

Kite Parrot

Knight Parrot statue,
Koolyanobbing

Kalgoorlie
Boulder
↓
x

Nerd Parrot seen
on internet all
night

x

2 AM:
Night Parent sees
young bird at disco.
↓

West Coast NP
on endangered list

x Perth

Tonight Parrot
seen - late
afternoon
↑

Last remaining
Bite Parrot taken
by Great Night Shark
(or 'Night Pointer')

1911: False sighting:
Fremantle Arts Centre.
Identified as Night Pirouette.

Nightie Parrot found
down back of drawers ↘
Albany
x

A HISTORY of SIGHTINGS

of the

NIGHT PARROT

POLYGONICUS INCONSPICUUS NOCTURNUS

The elusive Bearded Night Parrot has achieved legendary status. Recent near-sightings have inspired twitchers, scientists and ornithodontists worldwide to renewed efforts to make the much-sought-after confirmed sighting, or run over one.

Of these, Uncle Kev, former professor of Hydraulics at Northern Commando Training Academy, holds the current record for 'confirmed non-sightings and near-misses' and is founder member of the infamous Yarraville Mouth-Organ Orchestra. (YMOO).

roome

Earliest known sighting of N.P.
5AM, Thurs, 14th Sept.)

1948
Skite Parrot heard bragging about size of bill (at 'Budgies in the Park' restaurant)

Neat Parrot flock seen flying in straight rows

x 'Very late Afternoon parrot' seen, early evening 1867

CAUTION LOW SIGN

Kata Tjuta   Uluru

Burke & Wills' camel bitten by Night Parrot

Night Parrot
3AM, 30th Feb, 1947
Last known sighting:

← Tracks of the legendary 'Dotted White Lion' (a major predator of the 'BNP')

Mr. Sturt turned back by 'Dotted White Lion'

KEEP LEFT

x ←

← Bight Parrot shadow found, 1910

Bright Parrot sighted in headlights, August 1963

The Edge →

Where the Great Australian Bighted (Bit)

e Arid

For Kaye Keck

When we heard about Uncle Kev, we hopped straight on the train across the vast Nullarbor Plain to rescue him.

All the WAY to W.A.

Our
Search for
Uncle Kev

Roland Harvey

Uncle Kev

Bearded
Night
Parrot

←BACK

GREAT AUSTRALIAN BIGHT

At a secret location on the Great South Coast, we found our first exciting clue — a single dropping from the 'extinct' Bearded Night Parrot. We took this as a sign that we were already hot on the trail.

Someone yelled, 'Whales ahoy!' so we climbed out to the viewing platform, where the whales can watch people.

We found a cooking pot and the remains of scorpion curry. The curry was still hot... Uncle Kev couldn't be far ahead!

KALGOORLIE

We checked out Uncle Kev's quarry, dug in 1953 with the help of his friend Hugh Jarms. There was a rumour that the wicked Budgie Smugglers Society had been spotted in the area, but we didn't see anything unsavoury.

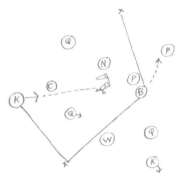

Uncle K Ⓚ put out bait Ⓑ in the form of succulent seeds dyed black to attract a bird of the night.

Trip wire Ⓦ alerted K Ⓚ to the bird's presence Ⓟ and he was shot by catapult Ⓒ carrying net Ⓝ .

Could Uncle Kev have found his quarry Ⓠ already, when we are only at the start of the book?

FREMANTLE

At the museum, a guard saw Henry making an exhibition of himself and threw him out.

We met an artist with a pet budgie, but he was of the opinion that the Night Parrot was probably just a budgie with a head-torch.

Penny had a Titanic moment on the submarine Uncle Kev used to command in his airforce days.

A photo in an exhibit at the musuem gave us a clue to Uncle Kev's movements.

COTTESLOE BEACH

The beach was full of sculptures! We heard some bits had gone missing. Dad guessed this had been the work of Uncle Kev, using spare parts to make a parrot-tracking device.

Frankie asked if he could join an ocean orchestra when he grows up.

We saw...

some lifesavers

a huge pencil

and some emus.

WRECK OF
THE BATAVIA

We followed Uncle Kev's trail to a low limestone island off the coast.

As it struck twelve that night, a terrible noise erupted outside our tent. Bones clanked, steel clashed and tortured souls shrieked...It was Dad, falling into the camping box.

Mum told us stories about the emu holding up the sky so we could go back to sleep. Frankie dreamed about sharks and dolphins, clear water and ancient pirate ships...

We found a pile of broken bricks...Could Uncle Kev have been practising his karate?

MONKEY MIA

We didn't see any monkeys or any mias but we fed bottle-nosed dolphins and lots of pelicans. A fish bit Frankie's finger, and he said he'd catch chips next time, too.

Mum's bottom... lip got sunburnt and Penny felt certain Uncle Kev was nearby, but we couldn't see him or any birds. We left seeds on the water just in case.

A dolphin did a pike with a double jackknife. Only Uncle Kev could have taught it that.

NINGALOO REEF

Henry saw 500 species of tropical fish.

Penny saw 220 species of coral and some very big fish, but we didn't see the whale sharks everyone was talking about.

Mum and Henry went out kayaking, and in the distance we thought we could hear Uncle Kev's creaky old pedal submarine, so off we went again.

A broken rubber band from Uncle Kev's submarine told us we were on the right track!

KARIJINI
NATIONAL PARK

At an amazing gorge we helped people make a holiday video and discovered that Henry can climb vertical rock cliffs!

Apart from Uncle Kev's wallet, and a note and an arrow, he left no clue to which way he had gone...

We found Uncle Kev's special north-finding compass — STILL POINTING NORTH!!! Cleverly, we headed off to the north-east...

THE PILBARA

On the road, Dad was worried we'd get bored so he made us activity sheets. But we were too busy drawing stuff and identifying tracks and poo and flowers and extinct species so we had to do our sheets after dinner.

Dad got right into his bush tucker guidebook. So far he has eaten green ants, poisonous seeds and worm castings. We collected 17 different feathers including one from a wedgie-tailed eagle. Penny spotted 17 different animal tracks, including a Pilbara lizard, and Dad got 17 different insect bites. Mum collected a bag of gemstones to polish, and Henry made 17 different colours by grinding clay into powder to make paint.

We saw 17 million budgies but no Uncle Kev.

Night Parrot, daytime

MARBLE BAR

At the Hottest Place on Earth it is over 37.8 degrees for 154 days of the year. Blue-tongue lizards and goannas and frill-necked lizards don't mind, but people can melt, especially if they're softish and a bit runny to start with. The rock is just grey, but when you wet it the colours really shine.

Dad cooked dinner on a rock and Mum made her special giant bonnet omelette, the Om.

On a rock, we found a solar-powered moustache-trimmer. We were HOT!

BROOME

At Cable Beach, we went out
on a boat to watch the sunset.

We didn't see any Night Parrots,
but we did see an Aussie camel
and some wise men. Mum
thought the wise women
were all out on another
boat, fishing for dinner.

We saw a bird that weighs less
than a handful of cornflakes
and flies 600 million kilometres
from southern Australia to
Siberia each year. (It is further
on the way back, because
it is in miles.)

Winter
plumage

FITZROY CROSSING

We were watching the footy at Fitzroy, starting to wonder if the naughty Night Parrot really existed, when a man who looked a bit like Uncle Kev's twin cousin came out of nowhere and kicked a heroic goal for the away team.

He had to leave before we got to speak to him...

So we all played kick-to-kick, and Frankie made a new friend.

We found Uncle Kev's lucky socks, running across the oval.

PURNULULU NATIONAL PARK

We hired a gyrocopter in the Bungle Bungles. The hirogyro man said someone had borrowed a 'copter yesterday, looking for some bird...

Were we getting close, or was this just another bungle?

We found some gyro-droppings:

Uncle Kev's Swiss Army everything,

mo-wax,

favourite book

and sardinofone.

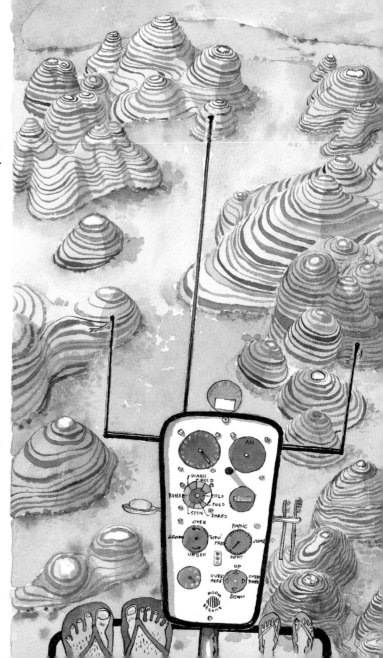

WYNDHAM

Right up north there were birds EVERYWHERE: darters, jabiru, Olga the brolga, and rainbow bee-eaters. We were so distracted we almost missed vital clues: a guide in a wooden canoe...another dropping...a lot of crocodiles and...

LOOK OUT, UNCLE KEV!

We found a Tait's GPS ticking inside a crocodile. He was swimming around in circles...

We couldn't believe it. There, before our eyes, were Uncle Kev
and his Night Parrot...wait, his two Night Parrots!

Uncle Kev introduced the one without the beard to the one with a beard,
and happily set them free. What a trip!

(Uncle Kevin is a fictitious character and not based in any way on any person, living, dead or almost. Especially Uncle Kev of Yarra Glen.)

On the Farm

CODE NAME: U.K

SECRET Nº:
2333333

TOE PRINT

TOP
U.K
SECRET DIARY

DATE: Today.

WEATHER: Fine, some snow. Chance of hurricane.

DAYS TO THE FULL MOON: 20
NUMBER OF CHICKENS: 31
DAYS TO MY BIRTHDAY: 14
DAYS TO MISS KELLIE'S: 23
EMERGENCY NUMBER: 33

After the accident I began to focus on regaining my strength, and teaching my local community the secrets of the Art of Survival...

iting helicopter.
incidental.
rge moustache.
llegible and a very
small red balloon.
lashed around the
anana.
xt? I had to think
ug. Alone, exhau-
hickens! One by one
bominable snowman
elting. Climbing through
ospital.

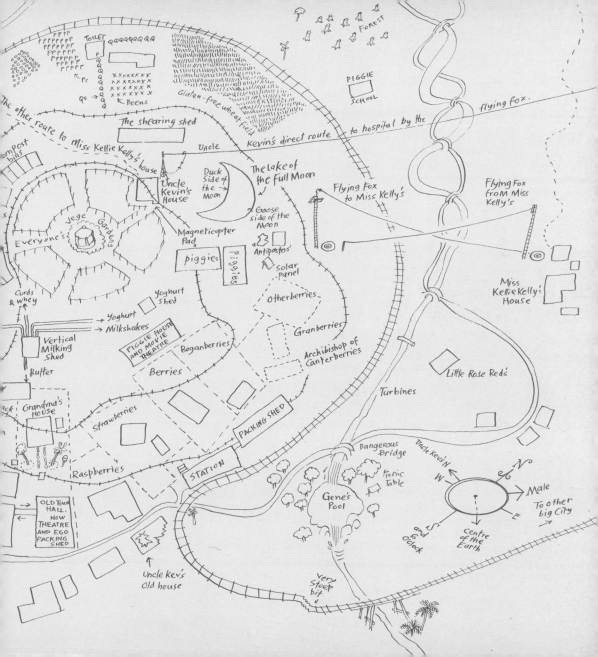

Dear Uncle Kev,
We are really looking
forward to our
holiday on your
farm!

loves Frankie
Penny
Henry
Mum
and
Dad

For Bob Brown

On the Farm

Our Holiday with Uncle Kev

Roland Harvey

I HAVE A FARM...*

Not any old farm. A working farm, where every animal has a job to do, and is precious, and nothing is wasted.

Where no job is too big, or too dirty, or too small.

Where no one is too rich or too poor, too old or too young, too important or too humble to share the work and enjoy the fruits of their labour.

Now, I'm sure we'd all like a nice hot cup of organic compost tea!

♪ Uncle Kevin had a farm,
A–E–I–O–U,
and on that farm he had a...shed,
A–E–I–O–U!
With a buzz-buzz here
and a snip-snip there,
here a snip, there a buzz,
everywhere a clang-clang.
Uncle Kevin had a farm,
A–E–I–O–U! ♫

*With apologies to Martin Luther King, Jr.

This is my SHED.

It is a busy place (especially since the Great Tractor Mystery) and in two weeks the Harvest Festival is on, so everything has to be ready.

I have a really good ,

and a tough old ;

a  is essential,

and a  as well.

And a

and a couple of , too.

I need to fix the

Luckily my family has arrived to help.

Henry Mum

Penny Dad Frankie

JOBS
GROW STUFF
FIX STUFF
PICK FRUIT
PLANT STUFF
TEACH PIGS
NEW SONG

TAKE YOUR PICK

WHEN LIFE IS
MESSING WITH
YOUR HEAD,

AND EVERY TRAFFIC
LIGHT IS RED,

AND YOU JUST
CAN'T GET OUT
OF BED ...

THAT'S WHEN
YOU REALLY
NEED A SHED.

OUR PLEDGE
We will grow
stuff and fix
stuff and
make stuff
and have a
good time

My friends Signor Paddy and Signora Maria Antipasto have chickens, ducks, geese, peacocks for the foxes and a wombat. Being vegetarians, they make cakes and biscuits and supply most of the eggs for the farm.

We are making 'The Hilltop Farm Cookbook' with Miss Kellie Kelly, who is also painting the pictures. It goes:

egg and lemon soup

Carrot cake

Sweet corn ice cream and garlic sauce

Miss Kelly, Miss Kelly,
my legs are like jelly.
I saw you yesterday,
and I didn't know what to say.
I'm writing you a letter,
which I have for want of better
judgement sent to you by airmail.
U.K.

BANTAMS
OF THE
OPERA

Dear Miss K

DOGS and FOXES!
BEWARE OF THE
PEACOCKS!

I spend some of my busy day polishing the piggies. They don't really need it, and they go straight back into the mud again, but I want to use my Pig Polisher invention.

Pigs are cleverer than dogs and humans, so I train them to do jobs and poo and make gas and compost for the farm.

♩ Oh...compost makes the garden grow, and methane makes the tractor go. ♫

They are also trained to round up the sheep for milking. You don't polish sheep, of course.

♫ A sheep is a sheep is a sheep,
  unless it's a goat, of course.
  You can milk it and knit it
      and count it to sleep,
          but to ride it,
       it should be a horse. ♪

I have three alpacas, Kerry, Alcatraz, and a baby, Alpacino, which probably means 'Little Alpaca' in Italian. On Sundays they have races against the ducks.

I have given Henry one of the most important jobs on the farm. He will be allowed to spread the poo in the orchard.

To do this he gets to drive the tractor.

I have let Dad try out the Bungee-Pik machine, even though it still has a few flaws. Mum is looking after Mr McCavity after his terrible bagpipe accident.

"I'm a fruit tree, I'm a fruit tree, I'm a fruit tree; that I am. But I'd rather be a fruit tree than a tram." ♪♫

♫ There are yams, yams,
    growing in our dam,
  on the farm, on the farm.
  There are yams, yams,
    growing in our dam,
  on Uncle Kevin's Farm! ♫

I got a letter from Miss Kelly today!

To show my good intentions, I am sending her a new piglet and some turnips.

I also built a solar mower. It works fine, except we don't have a lawn, so I'm converting it to a solar blender.

O. I would be in heaven,
my dearest Uncle Kevin,
if you would be my guestible
at the Harvest Festival!
                    K.K.

SHALLOW

DEEP

We can dry the grapes from our vineyard and make raisins and sultanas, but not dried apricots.

We make the grapes into juice, or put them on the table and EAT THEM!

And we freeze them and put them in our watermelon juice.

🎵 Some superheroes like to cook
cakes or marmalade or crepes,
but me, Uncle Kev, I wrote the book
on growing very special grapes.

I plant them out in special beds
where they can watch the cows,
and while they learn, I sing to them
and plant them out in rows.*

And I will stomp a special brew
with feet that aren't too smelly,
and wrap some in a ribbon blue,
and send it to Miss Kelly.

*pronounced 'row' in this instance

These are my Headquarters.

Many superheroes live in strange and complicated homes.
Mine is simple and functional.
I have taught the pigs basic housework and accounting.
The kitchen is my gymnasium, and I have devised exercises to keep me in peak commando shape.

Exercises include:

The Teacup Dip

The Toothbrush Calf-strengthener

The Fast Towel Shoulder Workout

The Straight-leg Sock Stretch

The Hammie Stretch

The Sit-up Comb

I have worked out, doing sums, that it is cheaper to have five horses than one car.

With five horses, you can do five jobs at once. And cars don't run on hay, or have baby horses.

Maisy is a Clydesdale and can pull a heavy cart.

Percy is a retired racehorse I am saving for Miss Kelly.

Zorro is a Shetland pony who is so fat she can't keep up with little Nell. She is always being naughty.

Sampson is having a foal. We might call him de Lilo.

Dear Miss Kelly,
I would love to be your Handsome Harvest Prince.
I shall wear my best Safari Suit if I can find it.
Or my Commando Ceremonials.
U.K.

Luciano's a little horse.

Concert Today Cancelled sorry

I am lucky enough to understand cows. They speak to me in Cow. (The boys just talk Bull.)

We have the happiest cows in all the hills.

♫ O happy, happy cowshed,
O fresh hay in our stall —
of all the creatures on Kev's farm
we're happiest of all!

Mmmmmmisty mmmmmilky mmmmooooorning,
mmmmmooooooonlight on the hill,
cooooooool shadows in the cooooowshed,
how quick our buckets fill! ♫

old cow   old cheese   blue cheese   blue cow

HAPPY COWS TASTY CHEESE

PLAN YOUR DAY

There's so much to do on these late summer nights before the festival.

♪ When the good ship Silver Moon
   sails its ocean o' twinkling stars,
   and tiny, tiny Pluto
   snaps the bright-red heels of Mars...

   We whisper to the carrots,
   sing sweetly to the peas;
   we bless the lovely broccoli,
   read poems to the trees.

   And if we see a shooting star,
   a blazing streak of light,
   we know that soon it will be a full
   and fruitful Harvest Night. ♪

Dear Mr. Kevin,
I've made you some chutney
from my best beetroot.
Will you wear for me
your ex-commando tie
and pale green Safari suit?
                        K.K.

Miss Kelly has been made Hay Inspector. She is also Library Assistant at St. Kev's School for Very Good Children, and paints teapots.

Miss Kelly thinks haybales stack better – but they won't win a prize at the local Sculpting Olympics!

I asked her to be my girlfriend and she said YES.

I was so excited that I called in a favour from an old friend...the Bearded Night Parrot*.

*Hint: He came all the way from W.A.

My most prized possession is my dad's car, Maurice. It is as old as he is. I love to sit in it and pretend I'm talking to my dad. Which reminds me — I'd better go and see if he's finished shearing the chooks.

Maurice is converted to run on chook poo and peanut butter. I have suggested Dad connects Maurice to the pumping machine so our shower works again. Meanwhile, he fertilises the kitchen garden just fine. Maurice, not my dad.

Every week the local kids come to help in the garden. They get their lunches straight from the farm! They can grow anything they like, and sometimes they win prizes.

At last it's here! To celebrate the big day, I have written an epic poem.

♫ Oh...Sydney has its Mardi Gras;
  in Melbourne there's a Moomba.
I'm not entirely sure at all
  what happens in Katoomba.

In Venice there's the Biennale,
  in Cairns it's Ukeleles.
But the one that's easily best of all?
  Uncle Kevin's Harvest Festival!

Well, Frankie picked the fattest grape,
  much bigger than his sister's;
and Mum made purple herbal cream
  for poor old Dad's sore blisters.

Penny picked five hundred flowers
  for all the neighbours' vases.
And Henry made some marmalade
  in pretty little jarses.

Miss Kelly wears a
shark-tooth charm, just
underneath her chin.
And me, Kev? I wear
a daisy chain and a
silly sort of grin. ♫

Thanks for the relaxing holiday, Uncle Kev!

love from
Mum, Dad,
Henry, Penny &
Frankie

Allen & Unwin
83 Alexander Street
Crows Nest NSW 2065 Australia
Phone: (61 2) 8425 0100
Email: info@allenandunwin.com
Web: www.allenandunwin.com

A Cataloguing-in-Publication entry is available
from the National Library of Australia
www.trove.nla.gov.au

ISBN 978 1 74331 367 1

Illustration technique: dip pen and ink; watercolour
Designed by Roland Harvey and Sandra Nobes
In the City, *All the Way to W.A.* and *On the Farm* typeset in Harvey,
created by Sandra Nobes from Roland Harvey's handwriting
Back cover illo from *At the Beach*
Title page illo from *On the Farm*
Imprint page illo from *To the Top End* paperback edition, © 2011
Colour reproduction by Splitting Image, Clayton, Victoria
This book was printed in July 2013 at Everbest Printing Co Ltd
in 334 Huanshi Road South, Nansha, Guangdong, China.

1 2 3 4 5 6 7 8 9 10

About the Author

Roland Harvey is one of Australia's best-loved illustrator. In 1978, he established Roland Harvey Studios and began designing and producing greeting cards, posters and stationery with a distinctly Australian flavour. Ventures into publishing quickly followed.

Roland's recent books include *The Wombats Go on Camp* and *Roland Harvey's Big Book of Christmas*. His illustrations also feature in *My Place in Space* (with Joe Levine, Sally Hirst & Robin Hirst), and the *Bonnie & Sam* series featuring the horses and ponies of Currawong Creek, in collaboration with Alison Lester.

Awards for the Series

At the Beach

Shortlisted, Picture Book category, Children's Book Council of Australia (CBCA)
   Book of the Year Awards, 2005

Shortlisted, Best Book for Language Development category, Speech Pathology Australia
   Book of the Year Award, 2005

Shortlisted, Picture Storybook category, YABBA and the COOL Children's Choice
   Book Awards, 2006

Shortlisted, Kids Own Australian Literature Awards (KOALA), 2006

In the Bush

Shortlisted, Speech Pathology Australia Book of the Year Award, 2006

Selected, *Magpies* Picture Book Picks, 2005

In the City

Notable Book, Picture Book category, CBCA Book of the Year Awards, 2008

To the Top End

Shortlisted, Picture Book category, CBCA Book of the Year Awards, 2010

Shortlisted, Lower Primary category, Speech Pathology Book of the Year Awards, 2010

Uncle Kevin's KEY To Wildlife

1 Tassie Devil, Wombat, Wallaby
2 Dolphin, Shark, Penguin, Whale
3 Glider Possum, Koala, Lyre bird
4 Wombat, Pelican, Eagle, Emu
5 Yellow-tailed Cockatoo, Emu, Kanga,
6 Sand Goanna, Budgie, Dingo
7 Finches, Eagle, Emu, Red Kangaroo
8 Frill-necked Lizard, Thorny Devil
9 Emu, Red Kangaroo, Dingo, Snakes
10 Green Turtle, Clownfish, Dugong
11 Green Ants, Butterflies, Cassowary
12 Dugong, Dolphin, Green Turtle
13 Saltie, Jabiru, Brolga, Turtle
14 Magpie Geese, Termites, Turtle
15 Uncle Kevin, Crocodiles
16 Night Parrot, Bite Parrot, Kite Parrot
17 Whales, Bight Parrot, Scorpion
18 Bilby, Dunnart, Echidna, Numbat
19 Quokka, White Pointers, Black Swans
20 Iron Emu, Wire-bodied Chook
21 Dolphin, Seal, Painted Button-quail
22 Turtle, Dugong, Dolphin, Bottle-nose Tourists
23 Whale Sharks, Turtle
24 Rock Monitor, Punk Emu, Rap Kangaroo
25 Budgerigars, Lizards, Wedgies
26 Emu, Roast Chicken, Red-faced Tourists
27 Aussie Camel, Saltwater Crocs
28 Freshwater Crocs, Freshwater Stingrays
29 Dingo, Geese, Purnululus, Emu
30 Jabiru, Darter, Brolga... Night Parrot?

We see Aussie Camel ㉗ Broom
Marble Bar seen from 48°c ㉖ ㉕
Marble Bar PILBARA
Damp here
Hottest Place on Earth
Where we found Uncle Kev's wallet
㉓
Ningaloo Reef
Karijini N.P. ㉔
No sightings ✗ of the NP here ✗ or here
㉒
Monkey Mia
Wreck of the 'Batavia' ㉑ Kalbarri NP
⑱ Kalgoorlie Boulder
Art at Cottlesloe Beach ⑳ Biggest dot on Australian mainland
Perth ㉚
'Night Pointer' ✗ Parrot sighting
Fremantle ⑲
Was King George Sound?